For Denise and Klaus

First published in Great Britain
by Andersen Press Ltd in 1994
First published in Picture Lions in 1996
9 10
Picture Lions is an imprint of
the Children's Division, part
of HarperCollins Publishers Ltd,
77-85 Fulham Palace Road,
Hammersmith, London, W6 8JB
Text and illustrations copyright
© Colin McNaughton 1994
Colin McNaughton asserts the moral
right to be identified as the author
and illustrator of this work.
ISBN 0 00 664520 8
Printed and bound in Singapore.

Suddenly!

Words and Pictures by
Colin McNaughton

PictureLions
An Imprint of HarperCollinsPublishers

Preston was walking home
from school one day when
suddenly!

Preston remembered
his mum had asked
him to go to the shops.

Silly me!

Preston was doing
the shopping when

suddenly!

He dashed out of the shop! (He remembered he had left the shopping money in his school desk.)

Preston collected the
money from his desk
and was coming out
of the school when

suddenly!

Preston decided to use
the back door.

On his way back to the shop
Preston stopped at the park
to have a little play when

Billy the bully
shoved past him and
went down the slide!

Preston climbed down
from the slide and went
to do the shopping.
He was just coming out
of the shop when

suddenly!

Mr Plimp the shopkeeper called Preston back to say he had forgotten his change.

Silly me!

At last Preston arrived
home. " Mum," he said.
"I've had the strangest
feeling that someone
has been following me."
Suddenly!

Preston's Mum turned around
and gave him an enormous

cuddle!

COLIN MCNAUGHTON was born in Northumberland and had his first book published while he was still at college. He is now one of Britain's most highly acclaimed authors and illustrators of children's books and a winner of many prestigious awards, including the Emil/ Kurt Maschler Award in 1991. *Suddenly!* was shortlisted for both the Smarties and the WH Smith/SHE Under-Fives awards.

SUDDENLY! by Colin McNaughton

"Colin McNaughton combines graphic finesse with comic-book slapstick."
Guardian

"Children will love this book"
Financial Times

Look out for more stories about Preston and his friends to be published in Collins Picture Lions.

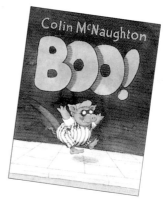